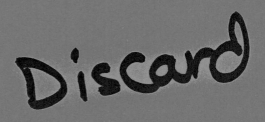

One Pizza, One Penny

First published in Chinese as *One Pizza, One Penny*

Written by K. T. Hao, Illustrated by Giuliano Ferri, © 1998 by Grimm Press, Ltd.

English language edition copyright © 2003 by Carus Publishing Company

All rights reserved

Printed in Taiwan

First American edition, 2003

The Library of Congress Cataloging-in-Publication Data for *One Pizza, One Penny* is available under LC Control Number 2003011127

One Pizza, One Penny

K. T. Hao
Illustrated by Giuliano Ferri
Translated by Roxanne Hsu Feldman

Cricket Books
Chicago

On Sunflower Street in Sunnyville,
  Ben Bear lived at number 14
  and Chris Croc lived across the way.
They were the best of friends.
And both were wizards in the kitchen.

Chris Croc was a baker of heavenly cakes.

Butter or berries, chocolate or cheese, raisins or
   honey or cream . . .

Eating Chris Croc's cake was like swishing soft
   clouds in your mouth.

It made you feel like stars were twinkling in
   your tummy.

Ben Bear was a maker of divine pizzas.
They had crispy crusts and fabulous flavors.
Eating Ben Bear's pizza was like swallowing a warm, soothing sun.
It made you feel like you were floating in the sky without wings.

Bear treated Croc to slices of pizza.
Croc returned the favor with pieces of cake.
They ate and they drank. They talked and they laughed.
Ben Bear and Chris Croc were the friendliest neighbors in the world.

One warm afternoon, the sun beamed tenderly down.
Ben Bear and Chris Croc were sharing cake and tea
   when a luxurious limo rolled up the street—and stopped.
Out stepped a chauffeur, tall and magnificent beneath his hat.
"Good day, sirs," he said. "Could you spare some cake?" he asked.
"Of course," said the croc, slicing the cake.
The chauffeur said, "Thank you. One piece is for me,
   and one is for my boss, Mr. Zhu."
Imagine that! It was Peerless Zhu, the legendary media tycoon!
Zhu owned six hundred publishing houses, and was the richest
   man on earth.

Peerless Zhu had a secret:
he was weirdly, wildly, fond of cake.
So great was Zhu's passion,
he had a special radar system in his car
   that could sniff out the aroma of cake
   for miles around.

The chauffeur swallowed his cake in a single gulp.
Peerless Zhu looked down his rather considerable
   nose.
"Cake like this must never be gobbled! You must
   admire its lovely design.
   You must sniff—ahhh, yes!—to take in the aroma.
   You must gently cut a sliver with a fork to feel its
   delicate texture.
   Only then should your mouth and teeth enjoy its
   exquisite taste."

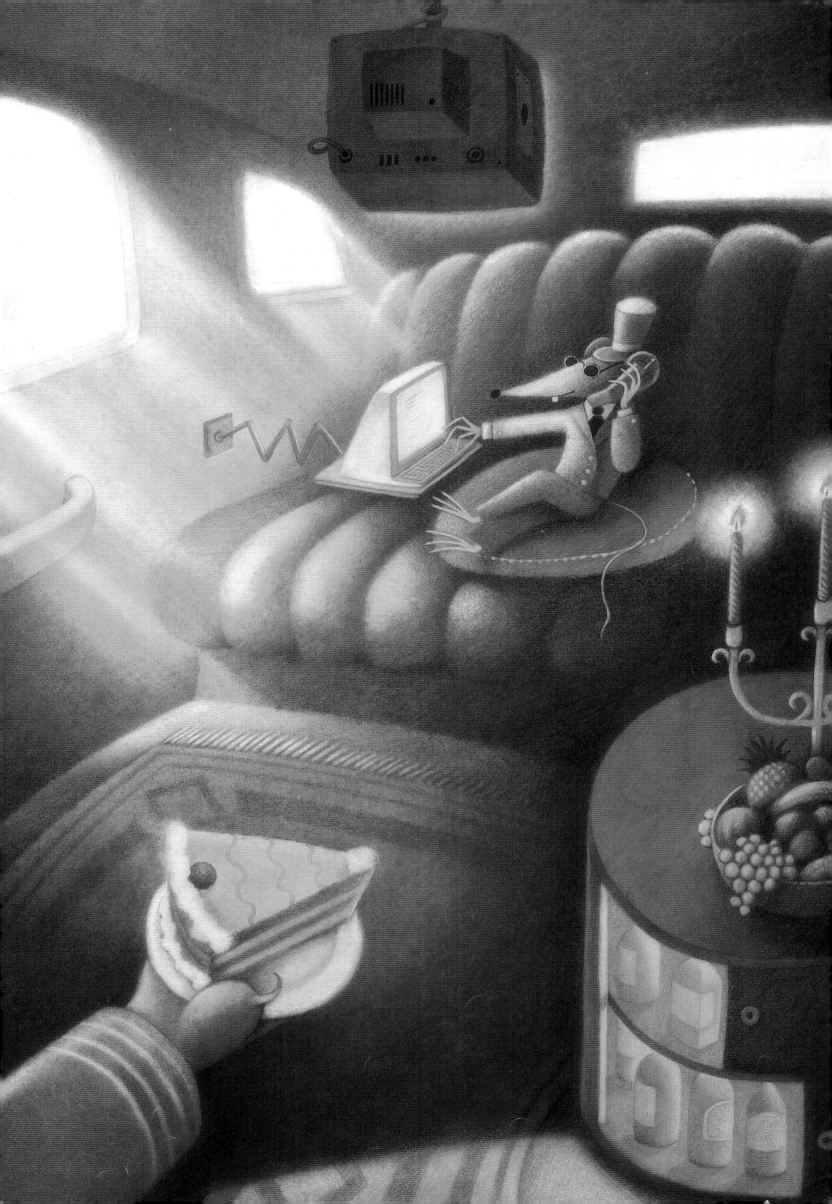

Peerless Zhu slowly ate his cake,
  enjoying every single bite.
He stared at the roof of the car and sighed
  with happiness.
Then he took out a gold coin and lightly
  placed it in the palm of the chauffeur.
He did not utter a single word. The chauffeur
  knew what to do.
The chauffeur gave Chris Croc the coin. "Here
  is a gold piece.
  Mr. Zhu congratulates you on creating the
  tastiest cake in the world."

That evening, gold coins kept jingling and
   jangling in Ben Bear's head.
Over and over he thought, "If Chris Croc can
   sell his cake,
   my pizzas can bring me a fortune!
   If each slice sells for one gold coin,
   and if I can sell 10 pizzas a day . . .
   that's 80 slices . . .
   for 365 days a year . . .
   Oh, boy! I'll be as rich as Zhu!"
Humming a tune, he set to work building a
   wagon.

The next day, the bear got up at dawn.
Still humming, he baked his pizzas.
As he pushed his cartful of pizzas down
   Sunflower Street,
   the sunflowers bloomed in brilliant gold,
   the color of money.

Suddenly, he stopped. What was this?

Chris Croc, sitting by the street corner,
peddling his cakes!

From morning till noon, not a single customer
  walked by.

Ben Bear was hungry. His stomach growled.

He asked his friend, "Could you give me a
  piece of cake? I'm as hungry as a bear!"

"Why can't you eat your own pizza?" asked
  Chris Croc.

"My pizzas are for sale," replied Ben Bear.

"My cakes are for sale, too!" retorted Chris Croc.

"But I don't have any money with me," pleaded
  Ben Bear.

Chris Croc was not sympathetic.

"Then, I'm sorry," he said. "No money,
  no cake."

By afternoon, Chris Croc was starving.

His head was spinning.

Black spots danced in front of his eyes.

If he didn't eat something, he would
waste away to nothing but a shriveled
crocodile skin!

He took out the gold coin Zhu had given
him and handed it to Ben Bear.

Ben Bear gave a slice of pizza to his first
customer.

Chris Croc swallowed it whole.

"Ahhh!" he sighed. "Like rain on a
sun-scorched field!"

Ben Bear saw the satisfaction
  on Chris Croc's face.
He could wait no longer.
He gave the gold coin back to the croc and
  bought himself a piece of cake.

Tightly Chris Croc squeezed the gold coin.
A single slice of pizza was not enough for a
  hungry crocodile.
He would buy another.

Ben Bear saw how much Chris Croc enjoyed
  the pizza.
So he bought another piece of cake.

That one gold coin flipped back and forth
  between those two
  until both of their bellies were full.

A crow dropped by in the late afternoon.
He wanted to buy some pizza.
"Sorry, sir, but my pizzas are all sold," Ben Bear
     apologized.
"Too bad," said the crow. "Then I'll buy
     a piece of cake."
"Oh, dear—my cakes are all gone, too," Chris
     Croc replied.
"Wow!" said the crow. "Your food must be
     delicious. Every last piece is gone.
     I'll come earlier tomorrow, and I'll bring
     all my friends!"

"Ben Bear, I must thank you," said Chris Croc.
"If not for your help, I wouldn't have sold
  all my cakes.
  And I spent just one coin in exchange
  for all that pizza."
"No, no! I am the thankful one," answered
  Ben Bear.
"Because of you, I earned some money today."

Ben Bear and Chris Croc pushed their empty
  wagons back down Sunflower Street.
Their first day of business had been a good one.
They promised to meet again early the next
  morning.
With lighthearted steps, they walked home in
  the moonlight.

Isn't it funny,
   what one gold coin can do?

K. T. Hao is considered the founder of modern children's literature in Taiwan. His renderings of fairy tales with a modern twist include *The King and the Nightingale,* and *Small Marbles, Big Troubles.*

Giuliano Ferri studied animation at the Art Institute of Urbino, Italy, and has illustrated many children's books, including *Noah's Logbook.* Ferri lives in Pesaro, Italy.

Roxanne Hsu Feldman grew up in Taiwan and is now a middle-school librarian at a private school in New York City.